THE ANIMALS' EASTER

'A king,' my mother said. 'One day you'll carry a king on your back.'

So I knew from very early on that I was something special. Not just your ordinary common or garden donkey born to live out his days as a beast of burden. I knew I was different from the start...

The little donkey has a surprise when he meets his special rider. But the first Easter was a time of surprises, and of sadness, and of great joy. You will find them all in these appealing and original animal tales which take a fresh look at the familiar Easter story.

AVRIL ROWLANDS is the author of many books for children. For Lion Publishing these include the very popular *Tales from the Ark* and its sequels and *The Animals' Christmas*. Among Avril's hobbies are swimming, walking, theatre and steam railways.

With love and thanks to Leslie Guest
for his enthusiasm, help and wise advice
in the writing of this book

The Animals' Easter

Avril Rowlands
Illustrations by Rosslyn Moran

LION
Children's Books

Text copyright © 2000 Avril Rowlands
Illustrations copyright © 2000 Rosslyn Moran
This edition copyright © 2000 Lion Publishing

The moral rights of the author and illustrator
have been asserted

Published by
Lion Publishing Plc
Sandy Lane West, Oxford, England
www.lion-publishing.co.uk
ISBN 0 7459 4158 3
Lion Publishing
4050 Lee Vance View, Colorado Springs,
CO 80918, USA
ISBN 0 7459 4097 8

First edition 2000
10 9 8 7 6 5 4 3 2

A catalogue record for this book is available
from the British Library

Library of Congress CIP data applied for

Typeset in 12/16 Zapf Calligraphic BT
Printed and bound in Great Britain by
Cox & Wyman Ltd, Reading

CONTENTS

To Begin...

It is said that animals are sometimes aware of things that people cannot see. In *The Animals' Easter* I show the events of Easter through the eyes of different animals who were there, or who might have been there at the time. Some of the animals in my book are mentioned in the Bible, such as the donkey who carried Jesus to Jerusalem, and the cock who crowed three times. Others I have invented. I have also, at times, blended the different Gospel accounts in order to simplify the story.

But *The Animals' Easter* is not simply another way of telling the story of that first amazing Easter. More importantly, it is a book about Jesus and the effect he had on the lives of those who met him.

1

THE OLD DOG

They say you can't teach an old dog new tricks, but that's not true. Well, not in my case. If I hadn't been able to learn a few new tricks after the Roman officer ran me down in his chariot, I would have been dead long ago. But I didn't die, although it was a near thing. As I lay in the middle of the busy main road in Jericho, farm carts and oxen missed me by a hair's breadth.

So there I was, lying in all the dust and muck, unable to move, just waiting for a heavy hoof or wooden cartwheel to finish me off. Then someone tripped over me. If it had been anyone other than Bartimaeus I wouldn't be here to tell the tale, for most people would have left me lying there. I wouldn't have cared either, the state I was in.

But as the man struggled to his feet, I remember looking up at him. I saw the coating of dust on his pale, kindly face, the thin red cut down his cheek where he had fallen against a sharp stone, and the milky whiteness of his eyes. I shrank back, expecting a blow, but he did not hit me. He just put out one hand and touched me gently on the head with his sensitive fingers.

Of course I didn't know then that he was blind. That was why he had fallen over me in the first place. He wasn't expecting a dog with two broken legs to be lying right in the middle of the road. Mind you, the way the Romans drive, it's a wonder the town isn't full of dead dogs, cats, even people! Always driving too fast, and never looking where they're going! But that's Romans for you. Act as if they're the rulers of the world. They are, when you come to think of it.

I must have fainted, for I don't remember anything more until I found myself lying on some straw. The same man was kneeling beside me.

'Where did you pick that up then, Bartimaeus?' asked a voice and, when I lifted my head, I could see an older man sitting at a table.

'I tripped over him.'

'Stinking mongrel,' said the man, but I was used to being called names.

'Try and drink,' said Bartimaeus, holding a bowl to my lips.

'You're wasting your time,' said the older man.

'I don't suppose he'll last the night.' But he was wrong. I'm a tough old dog and it'll take more than a speeding Roman chariot to finish me off.

So I became Bartimaeus's dog, and thanked my lucky stars every night for my rescue. One of my broken legs mended, more or less, so I could get around, although my running days were over.

My master used me as his eyes. We made an odd couple, him with his stick and me limping along on three legs, dragging my useless one behind me. I would growl to get him to stop, and bark to get him to turn right or left. Somehow I always knew where Bartimaeus wanted to go.

His friends used to make fun of us.

'Why do you keep that mangy old cur?'

'Picked him up out of the gutter, I suppose. Smells as if he ought to be thrown back there.'

Fine friends, I thought.

But my master and I didn't mind. We had an understanding, him and me.

We would spend most days begging. Bartimaeus was poor, just like his old mother and father. That was all right by me, for I had never known anything but poverty, and I had lived on the streets all my life. We would meet in the middle of town—the sick and the lame, the mongrel dogs, the mangy cats—and beg for coins or scraps from passers-by.

When we weren't begging, Bartimaeus and the others would moan about the Roman occupation, the rise in taxes, the price of fish and suchlike. I found it boring, but my master enjoyed it. He had many friends, for he was a good man, a kind man and he would help anyone worse off than himself. Many's the time he'd give away all he made begging. Anyone with a hard-luck story could rely on Bartimaeus, especially poor women or starving children. I couldn't understand why he did it, but then who was I to complain?

I slept much of the time. In the dust at the side of

the road, curled up round my master's feet, I would close my eyes and dream that I had four good legs and could run as I used to.

My master and I went on this way for some years. Me being his eyes and growing older and greyer. I didn't mind growing old with Bartimaeus, for hadn't he saved my life all those years ago? You've got to take what comes, I've found, and adapt and change. Like I said, it *is* possible to teach an old dog new tricks.

His old father and mother were upset by his blindness. 'I'd give you my eyes, Bartimaeus, if I could,' his father would say. 'I'd be happy to be blind if only you could see.'

And then Jesus of Nazareth came to Jericho. Word had been going round us beggars for some time. A teacher, he was called, and a prophet. Someone who was close to God. But I hoped he was a healer too, for that was what my master and I both needed. Healing.

'If this Jesus can make people well, perhaps he can make you see,' said my master's father, and he tried to persuade Bartimaeus to go and find him. But my master wasn't having any of it.

'Why should I be healed?' he asked.

'Because you're my son and I care about you,' said his father.

Bartimaeus did not reply, but I knew what he was

thinking. I always knew what was going on in my master's head. He was thinking about all those who were worse off than him. The ones who could not walk, or were too weak to hold up a begging bowl. The ones with terrible diseases which made them cry out in pain. Compared with them, he was well off.

So he never did go looking for Jesus. We heard all about him, though. Word soon spread through the town about how he healed the sick and made the lame walk. I pricked up my ears at that.

'Go and see him, Bartimaeus,' urged his friends.

But my master, who like me, has a stubborn streak, refused, although I knew that deep down he really wanted to meet this Jesus. He hated being blind almost as much as I hated being lame and, although you can get used to anything, the longing to be healed never leaves you.

On the day Jesus was to leave the town, he passed by my master.

You couldn't imagine a poorer, more down-at-heel bunch than Jesus and his friends. They were wearing plain, dusty robes and worn-out sandals. I wouldn't have looked at them twice if it hadn't been for Jesus. He was different. He was simply dressed and looked just as dirty and just as hungry and just as tired, but there was something about his eyes...

They were deep and dark, like pools of water. You

felt that those eyes had seen everything and known everything. And when Jesus looked at you, you felt he knew all about you, the bad bits as well as the good. It didn't worry me, although there had been a few bad bits in my life and I'd a few guilty secrets I'd rather no one knew about. His look just made me feel—happy. I was quite surprised. I'd not felt like that since I was a puppy, safe in the knowledge that my mother was there to fight my battles and protect me when I got into scrapes. I wagged my tail.

But Jesus had not come to see *me*, of course, and didn't look at me for long. He was looking at my master who was sitting huddled in his old cloak, for it was not quite spring and there was a bite in the air. Jesus looked as if he was waiting for something, but my master, who, as I've said, can be as stubborn as a mule, just stared blindly at the ground.

Then Jesus moved away.

'Go on, say something!' I wanted to bark. 'That was Jesus! Don't just sit there like a fool! Those that don't ask, don't get!'

Suddenly, as if reading my thoughts, my master began to shout.

'Jesus, have pity on me!'

Everyone turned towards us.

'Have pity on me!' my master shouted once more.

'Call him,' Jesus said.

Bartimaeus jumped to his feet and threw off his cloak. I got to my feet too. No one noticed me. But if my master was going anywhere, then I was going with him.

'What do you want me to do for you?' asked Jesus, looking into Bartimaeus's blind eyes.

'Teacher, I want to see.'

And he stood there waiting, with such a look on his face, hopeful and pleading all at the same time. A couple of tears spilled from his sightless eyes and ran down his cheeks. I felt a bit choked myself. I wanted to stroke my master's head as he had once stroked mine and tell him everything would be all right. I couldn't do that, of course, so I just crept closer and brushed his leg with my tail so he would know I was there.

Jesus was silent for a long moment. Everyone held their breath. The crowd, his friends, the beggars who had followed Bartimaeus across the road.

Then Jesus spoke. 'Go,' he said. 'Your faith has healed you.'

I looked up at Bartimaeus and, as I watched, the milky film that covered his eyes cleared away.

My master could see!

Jesus turned and walked off, as if he did not want to be thanked. He went up the road that led out of town and his friends went with him. Bartimaeus and

I followed. Bartimaeus walking tall and straight and looking from side to side as if he could never get enough of the sights he saw, although they were only the dusty streets and shabby buildings of the poor quarter of Jericho.

And me?

I went with my master, running proudly beside him on my four sound legs.

2

THE LITTLE DONKEY

'A king,' my mother said. 'One day you'll carry a king on your back.' And she spoke with so much confidence that I never doubted.

So I knew from very early on that I was something special. Not just your ordinary common or garden donkey born to live out his days as a beast of burden. I knew I was different from the start.

None of the other donkeys liked me. They used to call me names. They said I was proud. I didn't mind. Yes, I was proud. I was better than the other animals on the farm. I was proud that I had been chosen above all of them for this special job.

I had no idea *when* it was going to happen, of course. Neither had my mother. But it would happen. One day. My mother, who knows about these things had told me, so it had to be true.

I did not like being a donkey. If I could have

chosen, I would have been something else—a horse perhaps, like those they have in the Roman army. Tall and commanding. Donkeys are short and people think we're stupid. But we're not. We're very intelligent animals. So it was no wonder that I was going to carry a king. The only wonder was that it hadn't happened before.

'I expect it will start a trend,' I said to my mother. 'I expect that one day every king in the world will want to travel by donkey and we'll live in wonderful stables built out of marble and lie on beds of the softest straw and eat carrots and grass served on gold and silver plates.' I was very young at the time.

My mother nuzzled me with her soft nose. 'Where do you get such funny ideas?' she asked.

I got them, of course, from the camel. Where else? Not that the farmer who owned us was rich enough to have a camel, but one passed through our village from time to time. He was my friend. He had seen everything, and he told me all about the palaces he had visited. In return I told him about the king I was to carry one day.

'What do you think my king will be like?' I asked.

'I expect he'll be dressed in a robe of silver cloth, with a red silk cloak threaded with gold,' said my friend the camel. 'He'll wear a crown, of course— a golden crown which will gleam in the sun. He'll be

tall and commanding and everyone will shake with
fright in front of him and throw themselves on the
ground in case he's angry.'

'Why—what happens when he's angry?'

'A king's anger is like a thunderstorm, with rolls of
thunder and flashing lightning. It's a terrible thing.'

'I won't make him angry,' I said. 'I'll be quiet and
patient while he's sitting on my back. What does it
feel like to have a person sitting on your back?'

For no one had ever tried to ride me, not even
the children of the village. That was, my mother said,
because the king had to be the very first person

I carried. I felt proud about that, too, and did not mind the other donkeys being rude and stuck-up because the village children chose to ride them and not me.

'It feels good—if it's a good person,' said my friend the camel, 'and bad if it's a bad person who digs in his heels and beats you. But if it's a good person, you feel you could carry him for ever, to the ends of the earth.'

'What do you do if it's a bad person?'

The camel curled his lips. 'I throw him off in the desert and leave him to find his own way home.'

I wouldn't throw my king off, I thought to myself.

I had another question, but I didn't ask my friend the camel, for he would only have laughed. So I waited until I was alone with my mother and we were munching away at the coarse grass in the field.

'Mother. What is a king?'

Now that might sound a stupid question, but I had never seen a king and wanted to make sure I gave my first ride to the right person. It would be awful if I gave it to someone who wasn't a king, for the real king would be angry. I didn't want to face an angry king.

My mother thought for a while. 'A king is in charge,' she said at last. 'The ruler, the leader.'

'Like the farmer?' I asked. The farmer owned the farmland and all us animals, apart from my friend the camel, of course. He was not as I had imagined a king, for the farmer was bad-tempered and had black hairs growing out of his nose.

'No, not like the farmer...' she began, then thought for a moment, her head on one side. 'Although, in a way you are right. The farmer is the head of the farm. The king is the head of a country and all the people in it. He should make rules that are fair and be a wise person and care for his people.'

The farmer certainly wasn't like that.

We lived in a village called Bethphage. It was near the Mount of Olives, outside Jerusalem. The farm I lived on was a poor one and none of us ever had enough to eat. When I caught sight of my reflection in a puddle in the road, I was interested to see my bones quite clearly sticking out under my furry coat. I was small for my age, smaller than the other donkeys.

Although I was special, I was still expected to do my fair share of the work and it was a hard life. It was dull, too, but I was rarely bored, for I had my dream to think about. Sometimes I used to pity the other donkeys for not being born special like me.

I would dream about my king. He would be tall and bronzed and I would know when he was coming, for the air would smell different. Or if I did not know, my mother would, for she knew everything. My coat would be brushed until it shone like glass and I would stand in the field holding my head high. I would not need a rope to hold me while my king mounted, for I would stand still as a stone, and not move, even if he weighed as much as six sacks of corn. That was more than I could carry. And the king, helped by his courtiers, would sit on my back and it would feel good, for he would be a good king, not a bad one.

Then we would set off. I would try to give him a smooth, comfortable ride, walking round the potholes in the road, so that he would not bounce up and down. His subjects, who would be waiting for us to pass, would not want to see their king bouncing around like a sack of corn. And I would take him... where? Where would I take my king?

'To Jerusalem, of course,' said my mother when I asked her.

Jerusalem. Of course. I just hoped someone would tell me the way. It would be dreadful to get lost. He might be very angry and I wouldn't like to be lost and alone with an angry king.

Although it was not far away, I had never been to Jerusalem. But I had heard all about it from the old mare who lived on the next-door farm. At one time she had lived in the city. Dreadful, she said it was. Streets full of houses, people and carts, smells and noise. No trees to speak of, no green fields, no fresh air. Once was enough, and nothing would make her go there again. But the old mare was a sad old beast with a moth-eaten coat and squinty eyes. An old horse like that would not be able to cope with city life. I would.

Then, one day, while I was tethered beside my mother outside the house, two men entered the village. I had never seen them before, and did not take much notice. I thought they must have business with my master because they came straight over to the farm, but then they did a strange thing. They began to untie the ropes that tethered us.

'What's going on?' I asked my mother anxiously.

'Ssh.'

The farmer came rushing out. 'Here! What do you think you're doing! You leave those donkeys alone!'

'Are they trying to steal us?' I asked, but my mother only snorted at me to be quiet.

'Our master needs them,' one of the men said. 'He'll send them back.'

Well, that was really no answer at all, so I was surprised when the farmer just gave a grunt and disappeared inside the house.

I had no idea, of course, that this was to be *the day*. I mean, the men who came were very ordinary, dressed in brown homespun robes and grubby darned and patched cloaks. They certainly didn't look like men who had been sent by a king.

They led us out of the village and we saw a group of people walking towards us. I stayed close to my mother for I was scared. They stopped, and we stopped, and then my mother did an amazing thing. She knelt on her two front legs, right there in the dusty road.

'*Mother*,' I hissed, 'what *are* you doing?'

I was so embarrassed.

The men who had fetched us took off their dusty cloaks and laid them on my back. I began to panic. Then a man stepped forward from the group. Surely he was not going to mount me? He wasn't *my* king. He couldn't be.

I looked at my mother.

'Go with them,' she said calmly.

I looked at the man. He was hesitating, and I suddenly had the odd feeling that he understood what I was thinking. He seemed a nice enough person, I thought, but not a king. Where was his silver robe, his red silk cloak threaded with gold, his golden crown?

Then I had a dreadful thought. Perhaps, I thought, perhaps my mother doesn't know everything after all and it had all been a story—about my being special and chosen.

'I thought he was meant to be a king,' I said.

'He *is* a king,' she replied.

The man climbed on my back.

Having someone on your back felt strange. Different somehow from the sacks of corn I was used to carrying. I could feel that he was alive, while sacks of corn just hang there. He was not too heavy for me, either. He was—just right. I felt as if I had been carrying him on my back all my life. He was a good man, I could tell that. He did not dig his heels into my sides or beat me with a stick. He touched my head gently and I set off without thinking. I didn't even know if I was going in the right direction.

'Shouldn't he be dressed a bit more smartly?' I asked my mother, who was trotting beside me.

'Fine clothes don't make a king.'

'But he can't live in a palace dressed like that.'

'You don't need to live in a palace to be a king,' she replied. 'This king is a king of people's hearts.'

But I still didn't understand.

We had turned on to the main road to Jerusalem by now. And then a new thought occurred to me.

'How do you know all this?'

My mother smiled.

'A long time ago, when I was about your age, I carried a girl on my back. She was expecting a baby. It was winter. This baby, she told me, would be a king. Not of a single farm or a single country, but the king of all the world.'

'What happened to him?'

'You're carrying him,' my mother said. Soon she dropped behind me for we were approaching the outskirts of Jerusalem and it was difficult to walk beside each other through the crowds that were lining the road.

There were more people than I had ever seen in my life, which was not to be wondered at, coming from our small village. They were throwing down their cloaks, and tearing branches from the palm trees and tossing them onto the road for me to walk over.

Some were shouting and others were singing.

'Praise God! God bless the King who comes in the name of the Lord! Praise God!'

It was amazing! Nothing I had dreamt about had been as amazing as this. But it was frightening too. Now the crowds seemed pleased to see us, but what if they suddenly became angry instead? There were so many of them, running alongside, waving palms in our faces, staring up at us, pushing ahead. The palms felt strange beneath my hooves. I was frightened of slipping, frightened of knocking someone over. My steps faltered.

The man I was carrying stroked my head. Then he

bent down and whispered in my ear, 'Don't be afraid. I am with you.'

He was not any of the things I thought a king would be. He did not look as I had imagined a king would look. He did not behave in the way I had imagined a king would behave, but it didn't matter. For it was at that moment I knew that he *was* a king. *My* king. He took my fear away, so I lifted my head and stepped firmly and proudly on the cloaks and palms that lined the road, walking carefully to avoid the potholes, for I did not want my king to be jolted around like a sack of corn. Not because of what the onlookers would think, but because it was all I could do for him.

I wanted to carry him for ever, to the ends of the earth.

At last we entered Jerusalem and I took my king to the Temple. When I left him, I saw tears in his eyes but I did not know why. I only knew that there were tears in my eyes, too, and, as I went back home with my mother, the road seemed to shimmer in the late evening sun.

And I did not feel proud, just humble and grateful that I had been chosen, and I don't know why I was chosen, for I'm really quite an ordinary, rather stupid donkey after all.

But I had learnt so many things on that short journey. And especially, that camels don't know everything.

3
THE TWO PIGEONS

We were perched on a wall close to the Temple, watching the bustle below us. We were chattering about this and that, and whether we would build a nest together here in the middle of Jerusalem or in a tree farther out in a quieter part of town, when a man grabbed us by the neck and threw us into a sack.

Neither my bird nor I had noticed him creeping up. Mind you, we were in a particularly noisy spot, surrounded by people pouring into the city for the Passover festival. But I blamed myself, for hadn't it been drummed into us as young pigeons to be on our guard at all times and never, ever to hang around outside the Temple? It was just asking for trouble.

'What's happened?' squawked my bird.

'I've no idea.' That was not strictly true of course, for I did have a good idea, but I wasn't going to share it with my bird. She would find out herself, poor thing, before too long.

It had been such a lovely day until that moment. The great Temple, with its gleaming white marble, wide courtyards, long colonnades and fine decorations looked wonderful. Well, so it should. It was the building in which people worshipped God.

Our captor stopped walking and we were thrown, still in the sack, onto the ground.

'Are you all right?' I asked anxiously.

'I think so,' she said. 'Nothing broken.'

Not yet, I thought.

'What about you?' she asked.

'I'm fine,' I said, trying to sound brave and not think about my sore neck or what lay in store for us.

The sack was upturned and we were dumped into a small cage, already occupied by two other birds. One was a sleek, plump sort of fellow, the other old, thin and scrawny.

'Well, well, another couple for the chop,' said the scrawny bird drily. 'The bird-seller *has* been having a good day.'

The plump pigeon swaggered over and eyed us up and down. 'Wouldn't have thought you were worth the bother. You won't make more than a mouthful between you.'

'No need to be personal,' I said.

'You don't mean,' my bird whispered, turning

pale, 'you don't mean… pigeon pie?'

She shuddered and crept close. I put out my wing and she sheltered under it. I could feel her heart beating and felt an overwhelming rush of love for her.

'I wouldn't mind if they were killing us for food,' I said bitterly. 'Well, I would, but at least I could understand it. I mean, we've all got to eat, haven't we? But this is different.'

'What do you mean?' asked my bird. 'Aren't they going to eat us after all?'

I gave her head a gentle peck. She was very innocent.

'We're to be an offering,' the plump pigeon said in a know-all kind of voice. 'An offering to God. A sort of "thank-you" present.'

My bird brightened. 'I don't mind being a thank-you present.'

'You will,' said the scrawny bird.

'Why?'

'Because they kill us first.'

We all fell silent.

'It seems a funny sort of present to me,' my bird said thoughtfully.

'Oh, we're just for the poor people to buy,' said the scrawny pigeon. 'The rich buy bigger animals.'

'Does that make poor people's presents less important than rich people's?' my bird wondered.

Clever, I thought, and looked at her admiringly. Brains as well as beauty. But, to my mind, there were more urgent things to worry about right now.

'Do you think there's any way of escape?' I asked.

We all looked up at the wickerwork lid tightly covering the top of the cage.

'No,' said the scrawny pigeon.

We fell silent again.

'Why do people give presents to God?' my bird asked. The plump bird puffed out his chest, preened his feathers and cleared his throat as he prepared to give us a lecture. 'People give God presents for a number of reasons: to thank God for being alive, to ask him for favours, like a good harvest…'

'That sounds like trying to bribe God to me,' I said sourly.

'…and to say sorry if they've been bad,' the pigeon went on as if I hadn't spoken. 'It's their way of asking to be forgiven.'

I looked at him with dislike. He just had to show off.

'Wouldn't it make God happier if people just stopped being bad?' my bird asked gently.

Now that made a lot of sense to me, and I wondered why I hadn't thought of it myself. I was also beginning to wonder whether my bird might not be a bit too clever for me, which was a silly thing to

think about at the time. I felt confused, frightened and unhappy and flew to the top of the cage. My bird followed.

'It's just like a market,' she said, peering through the wickerwork. She was right. It was the biggest market I'd ever seen. The Temple courtyard was filled with pens containing animals, baskets of doves, pigeons, sparrows, and stalls where people could exchange their money for special Temple coins.

I don't think I had ever seen so many people—priests in their white robes, ordinary folk up from the country, merchants from the city, travellers from foreign lands, locals laden with shopping, sick and disabled people—and everyone jostling for space in the enormous outer courtyard. For a couple of small pigeons, it was a pretty frightening sight.

The noise was deafening, too, what with the shouts of the merchants, the bleating of the sheep and goats, and everyone talking, arguing and laughing at the tops of their voices. There was even music from a nearby group. At least, I supposed it was music.

I would have liked nothing better than to watch it all from a safe perch somewhere high up, out of harm's way. It wasn't the same, somehow, being a part of it. At least, not the part *we* were about to play.

My bird looked at me.

'If we are killed,' she said slowly, 'will it mean that people stop being bad?'

'I doubt it,' I said shortly.

'Because,' she continued thoughtfully, 'if it *does*, then, although I don't want to die, I suppose I *can* see some point in it all.'

I looked at her, wondering that she should have considered setting up a nest with me. She was far too clever, I thought humbly. And too good. I felt I had never really known her until now.

'It will be quick, won't it?' the scrawny bird said suddenly. 'We won't know anything about it, will we?'

'I just wish they'd get on with it,' said the plump

know-all pigeon. 'It's the waiting that's so bad.'

I looked down at them. The scrawny old bird was scratching on the bottom of the cage, muttering to herself, while the plump pigeon was trembling. I suddenly felt sorry for them, which surprised me no end. But we were all in the same basket, and fear does strange things to you.

A shadow fell across our cage. We looked up.

'How much for one bird?' asked a voice.

We could hear the clink of coins.

The scrawny bird gulped and looked at me with terrified eyes. The plump pigeon tried to stuff himself into a corner. 'It'll be me, I know it,' he moaned. 'I'm the fattest. Oh please no, I don't want to die, I don't want to die...'

My bird was beside me. I looked at her. She was so beautiful and I loved her so much that it almost broke my heart.

The bird-seller fumbled at the clasp of our cage.

What I did then surprised me even more, for I'm a very ordinary pigeon, quite as cowardly as everyone else. I flew into the bird-seller's hand.

Now, if I'd had time to think about it, I probably wouldn't have done it. I mean, no one sets themselves up to be sacrificed, not if they're sensible. But it was too late, for the bird-seller had tightened his grip around my neck.

And then it happened.

There was a loud cry as a man came running into the courtyard. Others followed.

'God's Temple should be a house of prayer!' the man cried.

The crowds were falling back, pressing against each other. The man ran to the pens containing the animals and unbarred the gates. Sheep, goats, lambs and calves, all rushed out and the man and his friends drove them to the gates.

If the place had been noisy a moment ago, now it was in uproar! Everyone was shouting and screaming and tripping over the animals. The priests and traders were cursing and shaking their fists, the poor people were cheering and waving. Children were lifted onto their fathers' shoulders, and the slow-moving sick and disabled people were in danger of being crushed.

'You've turned God's house into a den of thieves!' the man shouted, not seeming to notice the bustle all around him. He pushed over the money-changers' tables and their stacks of coins rolled across the smooth marble floor. The money-changers began shrieking and scrabbling about on the ground, crawling between people's legs to find their money.

All this time I was being held by the bird-seller, although I was struggling to get free. The other birds had flown to the top of the cage and were shouting and squawking. I couldn't do either, for I was being held by the neck, but I did let out a sort of strangled croak.

The man who had created all the havoc turned towards us. The bird-seller went white and let me go, and I fell onto the hard, marble floor.

'Take them out!' ordered the man. 'Stop making God's house a market-place!'

With trembling hands the bird-seller lifted the lid of the cage.

I didn't fly away with the others. I couldn't. I was bruised from my fall, and weak from being half-strangled. So I just watched the others go, one by one, up into the clear blue sky, the plump, know-all bird, the old scrawny bird, and my own beloved bird last of all, while I waited for someone's foot to finish me off, for who would bother with a common or garden pigeon like me?

But as I watched, the birds paused, circled, then flew back to the courtyard. And, as they approached, the man bent down, picked me up in gentle hands and tossed me high into the air.

I felt new strength. My wings flapped. Taken by the current I began to fly with my bird close beside me.

Soon we settled ourselves high on the roof, well out of harm's way.

'His name is Jesus,' my bird said, putting her wing round me, for she knew that I was still shaken. 'They call him the Saviour, for they say he saves others.'

I was too winded to speak, but I nodded my head, for my bird was beautiful and far cleverer than me and she knew about these things. And hadn't the man just saved our lives?

4

THE WORRIED CAT

When I heard footsteps coming up the stairs, I hid under a low table. There was nowhere else in the room I *could* hide for there was little furniture. I had jumped in through the window and should have jumped straight back out again, but I didn't have the strength. Besides, the smell of the food was so tempting I could not bear to leave.

So, I slunk under the table and curled myself into a small ball, which wasn't very hard, for I have always been a small cat. I was shaking with fright.

Let me tell you something of my story... I have always been a worrier. The cat who lives down the road says I worry too much. She says I should take each day as it comes, but I have never been able to do that. Anyway, it's all right for her—she lives comfortably, with plenty to eat, a nice place to sleep, and the odd mouse to keep her amused. Not like me.

My mistress is poor. Very poor. I have to work hard to keep her home from being overrun by mice and rats, and even then I get no thanks. My mistress is not a kind person.

So when I was expecting kittens, I was worried, for I knew my mistress would not want to feed any extra mouths. I was right. She didn't. Especially six extra mouths. She threatened to drown them so I took them away and hid them.

But that was only the start of my problems. I was very weak and needed to eat, otherwise I wouldn't make enough milk to feed my hungry babies. Where was I to find food? I couldn't go home. And in any case, how could I leave my kittens all on their own?

In the end I had no choice. I *had* to find food or we would all starve. So that evening I crept out of the stable in which we were hiding.

'Darling! How lovely to see you!' It was the cat from down the road. She was full of news.

'… It was such fun! Pity you missed it. The whole place has been in uproar! And all because of this man called Jesus. Do you know he stormed into the Temple, kicked over the money-changers' stalls and set free all the animals and birds waiting to be sacrificed? He saved them! During the Passover festival too! They say he's a king or something, but whatever he is, the chief priests are furious! They're searching for him everywhere. They want to arrest him and put him to death!' She stopped to take a breath and looked at me for the first time. 'But what about you? You look dreadful! What *have* you been getting up to?'

I told her.

'You can stop worrying,' she said. '*I'll* look after the kittens.'

'But I still need to find food.'

'You can stop worrying about that, too,' she purred. 'For I know where there's to be a meal with lots of food. It's in my house. But it's *terribly, terribly* secret...'

And that was how I ended up shivering under a table in my friend's house.

The door opened. From my hiding-place all I could see were feet. Dirty feet in dusty sandals. The hems of their robes were dusty, too, and fraying at the edges. I counted the feet. Twenty-six. That made… thirteen people.

They sat down and I was just wondering how long they would be staying and whether there would be any left-overs, when one of the men suddenly stood up.

I could hear water being poured into a basin. The man returned, knelt down in front of one of his friends and began to untie his sandals.

I was curious, so I crept out, forgetting to stay well hidden.

The man whose sandals were being untied was trying to pull his foot away. 'No Lord! I'll never let you wash my feet!'

I did not understand. Surely the kneeling man was a servant, for it was a servant's job to wash visitors' feet. He certainly looked like a servant, for he was dressed in a plain robe, with a towel tied round his waist and a basin of water at his side.

'Peter,' said the kneeling man, 'you don't understand. If I don't wash your feet, you'll no longer be a follower of mine.'

'Then wash all of me, Teacher—my hands and head too!' the man called Peter said eagerly.

'Anyone who has had a bath is clean, apart from his feet.'

I watched as he dried Peter's feet and then slowly moved around the group, washing everyone else's feet. The water in the basin turned grey.

'You are right to call me your Lord,' said the man when he had finished. 'And your Teacher. So learn the lesson I've been teaching you and do as I have done. Don't expect others to wait on you. Don't be self-important. Look after one another. If I am willing to be a servant, so you should be.'

He sat down and I looked round the pairs of clean feet. There was only one dirty pair now. Jesus' own. For this man, I realized, *must* be Jesus—the man who, so my friend said, they were calling a king. The one being hunted by the chief priests. The one they hated and wanted to kill.

I looked up at his face. It was a calm face. An untroubled face. But it was a sad face and his sadness touched my heart. I forgot my worries, I forgot my hunger. I even forgot my kittens. I crept back to my hiding-place.

Jesus thanked God for the food and drink. Then he broke the bread into pieces and poured the wine into a cup. As he shared the bread and wine with his

friends, he said, 'This is my body given up for you...' and then, 'This is my blood poured out for you. Remember this.' I didn't understand what Jesus meant, but I've never forgotten those words.

The meal began. Crumbs were dropped, but I didn't eat them. I had forgotten my hunger for I was too busy watching Jesus. He helped his friends to the best pieces of meat and poured wine for them when their cups were empty. He spoke to everyone in a kind way and the room was filled with the warmth of his love for his friends.

Now cats are loners and I've lived on my own all my life for I don't count the company of my mistress.

I've muddled through, fighting my own battles, worrying about this, that and everything else, but then that's my nature. The cat down the road is my only friend. But as I lay hidden under the table while Jesus and his friends ate and drank, I realized that I had never had anyone to love and that no one had ever shown any love to me. I had not known what love was until that moment. I stretched myself and purred.

But as the meal continued, I began to feel less comfortable. There was an atmosphere in the room. Something had changed... the very air was tense and I could feel my fur prickle.

When everyone had finished eating and drinking, Jesus looked round the group.

'One of you here tonight will give me away to my enemies.'

The room fell silent. Then they all began to speak at once.

'Who is it, Lord?'

'Which one of us?'

Peter nudged the man who was sitting closest to Jesus. 'John, ask him which one it is.'

'Which one of us is it, Lord?'

Quietly Jesus replied. 'It's the one to whom I'll give this bread.'

But I already knew who it was. Before Jesus had dipped the bread into a dish of sauce and handed it to the man sitting on his left, I knew. I could sense it. I had seen how the man's feet nervously rubbed against each other; how they were sweaty with fear. I could smell that fear. The air was foul with it. My fur crackled and stood on end.

'Be quick, Judas,' Jesus said.

Judas stood up and left the room. I could see the door opening on to darkness, for it was now night. It closed behind him.

I moved near to Jesus, and he put out his hand and stroked my head.

'Love one another,' he said to his friends. 'As I have

loved you, so you must love one another.'

I thought of my kittens. I felt calm and at peace. My problems hadn't gone away, but I felt I'd been given the strength to cope. I would find food and drink. I would feed my babies. They would live.

I looked round at the twelve pairs of feet in dusty sandals. Eleven pairs were clean, one pair was dirty. Jesus' feet.

None of his friends had thought to wash the feet of their master. But then a cat can't see into the heart of a human being, and everyone in that room had his own worries and his own sorrows to bear.

'Love one another as I have loved you,' Jesus had said.

So I put out my tongue and gently licked his dusty feet clean.

5

THE MOUSE IN THE GARDEN

I've always been a traveller. I've travelled the world—well, as much of the world as a mouse can take in. I've crossed the seas and seen strange countries and even stranger animals. I've fought giant rats on board ship, escaped by a whisker from many tight corners, and been chased out of goodness knows how many homes... I've had more adventures than I can remember. Oh I could tell you some stories if you've a day or two to waste. Some of them are even true.

But I've never stayed in any one place for long, for I've always thought that the grass would be greener in the next field and the food better. My friends say I have itchy feet. Not that I have many friends. 'Hello and goodbye', that's been my motto. I get bored easily, you see. So I've kept moving and never settled. I've never had anywhere I could call a home and it never used to bother me, but lately I've begun to wonder just what it is I'm searching for.

That night, the night it happened, I had been on a visit to Jerusalem. Now Jerusalem is a tense, restless city. I like that. It's an exciting place. It was the time of the Passover festival and it was full of people. There was plenty to see and plenty to eat, what with the food in the market and the scraps dropped by the crowds. But by evening, I'd had enough, especially after a narrow escape from a large and angry cat. So I left, to find a bit of peace and quiet and a place where a travelling mouse could rest for the night.

Before long I found myself in a garden. It was called Gethsemane and I'd camped there before. It was full of olive trees and there were nice dark places where I could hide from owls and other creatures who might be on the prowl for an evening meal. I found the odd twig and a bit of moss, made myself a comfortable bed in a crack between some tree roots, and settled down.

The stars, I remember, were very bright that night, the sky very black. The garden was bathed in moonlight and a slight wind set the silvery-green leaves of the olive trees rustling. I peered out from my hiding-place and, for a moment, felt overwhelmed—I suddenly realized that the world was very big and I was very small. It must have been delayed shock. That tussle with the cat had knocked the stuffing out of me.

And, for the first time I could remember, I felt lonely.

I wasn't lonely for long, however, for a group of men were coming straight towards my hiding-place. They were walking quietly and carried no lights. I lay very still. They stopped in a small clearing just short of the clump of trees under which I was hidden.

'Sit here and rest,' said the man who was leading them. 'I'm going further on.'

He beckoned to three of the men. 'Keep me company. I'm lonely and afraid.'

They followed him into the shelter of the trees and sat down, wrapping their cloaks around them. I was about to run away, but for some reason I didn't. They

were close enough for me to see their leader's face. In all my travelling I've never seen a more unhappy face, although unhappy is perhaps the wrong word. He looked anguished—full of pain and fear. I wondered if he had been hurt. Been in a fight maybe, like me with the cat. He moved a little way away from his friends, then threw himself face down on the ground. And now I couldn't have run even if I'd wanted to, for his arm rested on my hiding-place. I didn't want to disturb him by running across his hand.

He spoke.

'Father,' he said. 'My Father. Please—if it's possible—take this terrible suffering away from me!'

I wondered, at first, who he was speaking to. Sweat was pouring down his face. He was silent for a while, then groaned aloud, but soon spoke in a calmer voice.

'But don't do what *I* want. What *you* want is all that matters.'

I knew, then, who he was, for I'd been staying around Jerusalem for a few days. I'd scuttled through the mass of people that had lined the route to cheer him as he entered the city on a donkey. I'd gone with the crowds to the Temple and watched from a hole in the wall as he released the animals and birds. But I'd known about this man anyway, long before that day. For I was a traveller, and stories about him had spread far and wide. How he healed people and talked to them about God. How he was chosen by God to make people kinder to one another. How he had come to save others.

His name was Jesus. He was called other things too. Lord. Saviour. King. Some people were even saying that he was God's Son.

'Father!' he called. 'My Father!'

He was silent for a while, and I almost nodded off to sleep. But I woke when he stood up. He went over to his friends. 'Peter, James, John, are you asleep?'

They sat bolt upright, rubbing their eyes. They looked ashamed.

'Aren't you able to stay awake with me for just one hour? You need to pray, too.'

But even as he walked away, their heads were nodding and their eyes closing. I could not blame them for I was tired myself. Jesus prayed again, then, for a second time he woke his friends, but they were soon fast asleep once more.

Jesus threw himself down by my hiding-place. He was silent for a long while but his lips were moving. I crept closer and closer until I could feel his breath stirring my whiskers. His eyes were shut but, as I watched, tears began to force their way past his closed lids and run down his cheeks. A drop or two even fell on me, but I didn't mind. I stayed as still and as quiet as I could. His whole body shook with sobs.

Now I was shaking too. But not from cold. I was shaking in sympathy. I felt so sorry for him. I wanted to comfort him, to tell him not to be afraid, not to feel lonely. I *cared* about him, which was odd, for I'd never cared for anyone other than myself. But I cared about Jesus.

'My Father, if you want me to go through this suffering, then I will,' he said out loud.

I looked at the dark shapes of the sleeping men. The world seemed to be sleeping, too, with only the two of us still awake. My eyes felt heavy so I rubbed them and blinked hard. I would not sleep. If all

I could do was watch and wait with Jesus, then I would do it. The fact that he'd never know made no difference. I couldn't leave him alone in the dark that night. Someone had to stay awake, to share his suffering, even if it was a homeless and friendless middle-aged mouse. A travelling mouse who was searching for something and didn't even know what it was.

An owl hooted, but I didn't try to hide. I felt safe. Protected. Dark shapes of moths flew by on silent wings and there was a rustle in the undergrowth where some animal was prowling in search of food.

'Father,' Jesus called. 'My Father!'

He sat up and saw his friends. For a third time he went over to them.

'Are you still sleeping? Look! The time has come. Get up and let us go.'

I dived into my hiding-place for the olive grove was suddenly alive with dancing lights, the tramping of feet, the sound of voices. I heard shouted orders and suddenly a troop of soldiers and a crowd of rough-looking men with swords and clubs burst into the clearing.

Jesus' friends leapt to their feet and stood around him. They were dazed with sleep, bewildered and terrified.

'Look,' Jesus said, 'here comes my betrayer.'

He pointed, and I saw one of the men who had come with the soldiers step forward.

'Teacher,' the man said. 'Peace be with you.' And he kissed Jesus.

'Are you betraying me with a kiss, Judas?' Jesus asked sadly. He turned to the soldiers. 'I'm the one you want, so let these others go free. But why have you brought all these men to capture me as if I was a dangerous criminal? You could have arrested me at any time during the day when I was teaching in the Temple.'

Now Jesus' voice sounded different. I crept closer and looked into his face. There was no sign of tears, no sign of the anguish he had been through. Now he looked sad but calm.

His friends weren't so calm though. One of them drew his sword and rushed forwards. Jesus stopped him.

'That's enough, Peter! Put away your sword. If I wanted to escape, I could call to my Father and he would send armies of angels to my rescue. But that's not God's plan.'

The officer in charge barked out an order. Soldiers surrounded Jesus and bound his hands. Then they took him away. His friends looked at one another, their faces full of fear. Then they turned and fled, scattering into the darkness of the trees.

It was quiet now in the garden. The owl had been scared away by the noise, and so had the moths and the animal that had been searching for food. I looked up. Even the moon and the stars seemed to have fled away and a few spots of rain began to fall out of the cloud-covered sky. They fell on me just as Jesus's tears had done. The sky itself seemed to be weeping for him, just as I had.

But the garden was peaceful now, silent and dark. Everyone had gone.

Except me. I stayed, for I was tired of travelling. There was nothing more I could do for Jesus, but I had found what it was I had been searching for. I had found peace. And a home—in the garden of Gethsemane.

6

THE COCK THAT COULDN'T CROW

I was perched on a branch of a tree on the Mount of Olives when I first heard him speak.

'Peter, before the cock crows twice, you will say three times that you don't know me.'

That was what the man said. I flew to a lower branch in order to hear better.

'I'll never say that!' Peter exclaimed. 'Even if it means dying with you!' He seemed very upset.

What wouldn't I have given to crow just once, let alone twice, I thought. But the man couldn't have meant me. He didn't even know I was there. I knew who *he* was, of course. His name was Jesus. Everyone who lived in the high priest's house knew him, for our master said he was a trouble-maker. Funny. He didn't look like a trouble-maker to me. I'd also heard that he was a prophet, able to foretell the future, but if he was a prophet he would have known that it was no use expecting me to make *that* prophecy come true. It was two years since I had last been able to crow.

Two years. Two long years since I'd stood in the courtyard of the high priest's house, ruffled my tail feathers, opened my mouth and breathed in the fresh morning air. And what had happened? Nothing. I couldn't believe it. A cock who couldn't crow. It was like a bad joke, but I can't say I was laughing.

I can remember as if it were yesterday how I tried and tried, only stopping when I felt dizzy. And how the word spread among the hens, *my* hens, who had always looked up to me. They had cackled with laughter and said hurtful things, but they were right. What good was a cock that couldn't crow? How would anyone know when it was daybreak and time to get up? I had woken the household for so many years. What would they do now that I had no voice? They might decide I was no longer worth feeding. They might even kill me. The thought was frightening, but it was the shame that was hardest to bear. I had always been the most important bird in the household and I couldn't endure the disgrace.

My life changed on that dreadful day and has never been the same since. Imagine it. Two years of seeing my hens desert me for younger cocks who could crow sweetly in their ears. Two years worrying every time the cook came into the courtyard with a knife. I was a shadow of my former self. I used to have a fine coat and glossy feathers, but not any more. I was so unhappy that at last I decided to leave the high priest's house. I didn't know where I would go. I didn't even care if a fox caught me.

So that was how I came to be sitting on the branch of the olive tree and heard Jesus' words.

I didn't stay to hear any more and was in a thoughtful mood when I fluttered down from the tree and returned to my home in the high priest's house.

Why did I return to my old home? Simple. Because I'm a coward. I had never been away before, and the world beyond the high priest's house, the bare rocks, the vultures wheeling overhead, was frightening. It was all so different from my comfortable home with its endless supplies of food and water, its pleasant courtyards, paved walks and well-stocked gardens. Better, I thought, to be miserable in comfort than die alone in some horrible place. So, as the light faded, I returned to the only home I knew and crept into my nesting place. No one had even noticed I had gone. And I used to think myself so important and such a fine, brave creature. It was very humbling.

Some hours later there was a commotion at the gate. I had not been able to sleep and quite welcomed the disturbance. People were arriving and I recognized some of them. Priests, teachers, elders of the Temple. Normally quiet and dignified, these religious men seemed unusually excited. There was a good deal of bustle. Lights were kindled, servants roused from sleep, much rushing to and fro with smoking torches and jugs of wine. Someone lit a fire in the middle of the courtyard so I knew that the fuss, whatever it was, would go on for some time. I flew to the entrance. A troop of soldiers was approaching, followed by a fair-sized crowd from the town. The soldiers clumped in through the gates, and I almost missed the man

they were guarding. But someone hurried over with a torch and in its flickering light I saw that the prisoner was Jesus.

His hands were tied and the soldiers were crowding closely round him. But he didn't seem to notice their jostling. He was looking around and, for an instant, I swear he caught my eye.

Jesus was brought into the courtyard. The high priest had come out of the house by now and the crowd pressed forwards. I stayed well out of harm's way, keeping in the shadows by the wall. Suddenly I saw a man slip through the gates. His cloak was tightly wrapped about him, his head bent as if he didn't want to be seen. But I knew him. It was Jesus' friend, Peter. Once inside, he made his way over to the fire.

By this time the soldiers had pushed Jesus in front of the high priest. They forced him to his knees. The priests began to question him and, all the while, Peter sat silent, head down, arms outstretched to the fire. But I could see that his hands were shaking.

Jesus answered their questions simply and without fear. I wondered, as I watched him, how he could be so brave.

Hours passed. It was the blackest part of the night. The courtyard had grown much quieter. The hens had gone back to their roosts, the fire had died down and the people and dogs lying round it had dozed off. Peter was still awake however, his hands held out to the warmth, his eyes fixed on the glowing embers, his body tense, straining to hear the voices that continued to question his friend. And I too was awake, unable to go to my roost and sleep.

A servant came into the courtyard. As she approached the fire she caught sight of Peter.

'You're one of them,' she said. 'You're one of Jesus' friends.'

Peter raised his head. He looked terrified.

'No,' he said. 'No I'm not. I don't know what you're talking about.'

A little later another servant came out and said to one of the men standing with Peter, 'This man *was* with Jesus.'

But Peter insisted, 'No, I wasn't. I don't know anyone called Jesus.'

Across the courtyard there was a sudden commotion. The High Priest stood up. He raised his voice.

'Are you the Messiah, the Son of God?'

There was a moment's silence. I held my breath. Jesus replied.

'I am.'

The courtyard was in uproar. Everyone jumped to their feet, shouting, hurling abuse, shaking their fists. The high priest tore his robes in his rage.

'We don't need any more witnesses,' he thundered. 'He's condemned out of his own mouth! What is your verdict?'

'Death!' they yelled. I shivered. The people asleep by the fire woke with a start. Dogs began to bark, cats miaowed, hens fluttered down from their roosts, soldiers sprang to attention. Fresh lights were kindled and charcoal thrown on the fire. Flames spurted up. The soldiers began beating Jesus and made fun of him.

'Who hit you? Go on! You're the prophet. Guess!'

Jesus was silent.

Now I've lived all my life in the High Priest's house and seen many men brought in for questioning, but no one behaved with more dignity than Jesus. He did not speak as the soldiers beat him, nor did he cry out. That made them more angry, so they hit him even harder and, when they had finished, it was the crowd's turn to spit on him and beat him with the sticks they had brought. I thought they would tear him to pieces. I turned away, for I could not bear to watch. People can be so cruel.

Hearing the uproar, Peter jumped to his feet. Another servant stared at him.

'You *are* one of them,' he said loudly. 'You're a friend of Jesus of Nazareth.'

'I'm not,' Peter insisted. 'I don't know what you're talking about!'

'Of course you are. You can't deny it. Your Galilean accent gives you away.'

'I *swear* I'm telling the truth!' Peter shouted. 'May God punish me if I'm not. I don't know that man!'

More soldiers came pushing past to take Jesus away and I flew up onto the wall. A fresh wind blew in my face, and, on the far horizon, I could see the first faint streaks of day. The long night was nearly over.

I took a deep breath.

Then, unbelievably, my voice echoed round the courtyard, filling it with sound, stilling the cries of the crowd. *My* voice. I faced the dawn and proudly lifted my chest. I crowed once. Twice…

I turned towards the courtyard. And it was only then that I remembered Jesus' words.

I saw him being taken away. His clothes were torn. His face was bruised. He was bleeding from the many cuts he had received. But his walk was upright and his face calm.

He looked at Peter. Not an angry look, nor reproachful. A look of pity and understanding.

Peter caught his breath. He turned pale and I thought he might faint. Then he bowed his head and pushed his way blindly through the crowds, tears streaming down his face as he ran out of the courtyard.

And I felt for him, for I knew what it was like to feel ashamed. I too was a coward.

Then they were gone. The soldiers, the people, the priests, the servants. The courtyard was empty and I was left alone to welcome the new day with my new-found voice.

7

THE ROMAN HORSE

As soon as we'd received our orders, we left the stables. We didn't question them. Of course we didn't. Soldiers and their horses don't ask questions. They obey. That's the way we've been trained. If you ask questions, you don't last long in the Roman army. So when we were summoned to the governor's palace and told to look sharp about it, we did just that.

'What's up?' asked the horse who cantered beside me. 'Why the hurry?' He had only recently arrived from Rome and didn't know what had been happening.

'There's talk of a riot,' I said. 'There's always the danger of riots at festivals. They've arrested a Galilean called Jesus. Apparently he's been going around saying he's a king, although some of the people are saying that he's more than a king. They're saying he's the Son of God, and it's upset their priests no end.'

Now I knew all this because my master was the officer in charge. Besides, I made it my business to keep myself informed.

I snorted. 'There're always hotheads trying to stir up trouble and if they're allowed to get away with it, the next thing you know is that there's a revolution and everything will get in a terrible mess.'

I knew what I was talking about for I had seen it happen time and time again. I was all for order and discipline, for that was the way we had been trained in the Roman army, and our army had conquered the world.

When we arrived at the palace, we found a large mob of people milling round the steps. Foot-soldiers were trying to keep them back, and not making a very good job of it, I might add. But once *we* appeared, the crowds soon shifted.

Jesus, the prisoner, was standing in front of the Roman governor. He didn't look wild or dangerous. In fact he looked very ordinary, but then looks aren't everything. His hands and feet were bound in chains and he was bruised and bleeding from being beaten, but he held himself upright.

'Are you the king of the Jews?' asked Pontius Pilate, the governor.

'So you say,' Jesus answered.

His reply made the crowd very angry. They started shouting.

'Don't you hear what they're accusing you of?' Pilate asked. Jesus did not speak. I admired his courage, for it takes courage to stay silent when a crowd is baying for your blood.

'What will happen now?' my companion asked.

'It's a custom at the Passover festival for the governor to free a prisoner,' I told him. Romans

always supported local customs—provided, of course, that they did not conflict with the interests of Rome.

'So they'll free Jesus then?' my companion asked, but I wasn't too sure about this, for crowds can be fickle.

Sure enough, led by the priests, this crowd had begun to chant, 'Barabbas! Barabbas! Free Barabbas!'

I must say I was surprised. Barabbas was a thoroughly nasty piece of work, a real trouble-maker, who had led us a fine dance until we'd captured him a few days earlier. He was a murderer and an out-and-out villain and I for one would have been glad to see him hung on the cross. Yet now the crowds wanted him freed!

Then the priests led the cry against Jesus.

'Crucify him!' they yelled.

The crowds took up the cry. 'Crucify! Crucify him!'

The governor shrugged. I could see he didn't like it. 'But this man has done nothing to deserve death!'

That only made matters worse. The shouts grew louder and the people began to push and shove. We were hard put to keep the line and prevent them rushing up the steps to the palace.

The governor knew when enough was enough. Well, he would. Any good Roman general knows that sometimes you have to retreat. He called for a bowl of water. 'I'm not responsible for the death of this man,' he said, and washed his hands in front of them. 'This is your doing.'

So Barabbas was set free, and the people hoisted him onto their shoulders as if he was a hero rather than a murderer. But there's no accounting for people, as I've found out from my years in the army.

'What do we do now?' asked my companion.

'Go back to the barracks once the crowds have gone,' I said.

But the crowds didn't go. They stayed while Jesus was beaten once more, shouting their approval each time the whip came down. They roared when one of the governor's soldiers made a crown out of thorny twigs and rammed it down on his head. They shrieked with laughter when a stick was put in his hand and a scarlet robe round his shoulders and the soldiers bowed down saying, 'Long live the King of the Jews!' I had heard that kind of cruel laughter before and felt cold, although the morning was well advanced and the sun beat strongly on my back.

And Jesus still said nothing. His quiet dignity earned my respect and I was sorry he had to die.

We were ordered to accompany the priests and the condemned man through the town. The streets were crowded and it was a job to force our way through. Some of the people shouted insults, some were silent, others wept. It was a slow procession, for Jesus could barely manage the heavy wooden crossbar he had to carry. At last my master grabbed hold of a stranger and forced him to help.

'I've never seen a crucifixion before,' said my companion uneasily.

I glanced at him. He was young and not long out of training. I felt sorry for him.

'It's not a pretty sight,' I said. 'But if you stay in the Roman army, you'll see far worse, so you'd better get used to it.'

Two other men were to be crucified at the same time, two robbers, but no one paid them any attention, for everyone was looking at Jesus as he made his painful way through the crowded streets.

Suddenly he looked at me. It was a strange look for a man on his way to die. It was as if he knew what I was feeling and wanted to tell me that it was all right, that it wasn't my fault. And I knew then, without a shadow of doubt, that he *was* innocent of the charges they'd laid against him. I think I'd known it all along. But orders are orders, and if you're a horse in the Roman army you obey if you know what's good for you. So I steeled myself and rode steadily on to the place of execution, which they called Golgotha.

All too soon we were there and the three men were stripped of their clothes and nailed to the crosses.

The crosses were raised and the men left to die, while we lined up to form a barrier to make sure no one tried anything stupid.

As I said, it wasn't a pretty sight, but I'd seen it all before and I knew that we had to make examples of criminals. Except that Jesus wasn't a criminal.

The two men crucified with him cried out in agony and the crowds laughed.

But Jesus said nothing.

I'll never forget the scene. There was a small group of women weeping at the foot of the cross. A man was trying to comfort them, but he was weeping too. I looked away. The three crosses, with the figures hanging from them, were dark against the deep blue sky. The hot sun was beating on my back. My mouth felt dry with dust. There were flies everywhere. I tossed my head but there was no escaping them. The whole place stank, for Golgotha was the waste tip for the town. And although I tried not to, I couldn't help thinking about the agony Jesus must be in, the pain of his wounds, the burning sun, the dryness, the dust, the flies.

And still they wouldn't leave him in peace. 'Aren't you supposed to be God's Son?' someone shouted.

'Then prove it by coming down from the cross!'

I don't know why I was so troubled. Yes, he was innocent, but I'd seen innocent men die in the past. Men make mistakes and if his death stopped more people being killed, didn't that make it right? But no. It didn't.

I raised my head. High above me Jesus looked down.

I'll never forget that look as long as I live. It went straight to my heart. It was a look full of love. It was as if he was saying to the crowds, to the chief priests, to the soldiers, even to me, a tired old warhorse in the Roman army, 'It doesn't matter what you do. You can

torture me, kill me, whatever you like. *Nothing* will stop me from loving you.'

My eyes blurred until all I could see was the outline of the cross.

Now I'm an old horse and I've seen it all before—battles, riots, beatings, crucifixions. I've tried to do my duty and be upright and disciplined. I've been loyal to three things—my master, my legion and my country—and I've never doubted any of them. It takes a lot to shake me, but that look of Jesus' shook me and, for the first time in my life, I questioned what I was doing. I wondered why we were killing this good man. And I also wondered whether the stories about him were true. I think my master was wondering too, for I felt him shift uneasily in the saddle.

Then Jesus spoke.

'Father. Forgive them, for they don't know what they're doing.'

I bowed my head in shame.

It took three hours for him to die. Some of the foot-soldiers passed the time playing dice and tossing for Jesus' clothes, but we could only watch and wait under that brilliant, burning sun.

But I no longer minded the heat or the thirst or the flies. I stood as firmly as only a trained army horse can stand. If Jesus could bear it patiently, then so could I.

Suddenly the light faded. The crowd, who had fallen silent, began to murmur. I heard a whinny and glanced around. Although it was still mid-afternoon, it had grown so dark I could only just make out the shape of my companion's tossing head and his white, rolling eyes.

'Is there going to be a storm?' he asked fearfully.

Before I could speak, there came a terrible cry from the cross.

'My God! My God! Why have you left me?'

I looked up, straining my eyes, but could see nothing. Jesus spoke again. 'It is finished!'

And then, in the darkness, he died.

My master, who had sat upright on my back throughout, gasped, sagged in the saddle and almost fell.

'That man,' he said, 'really was God's Son.'

And as I carried him back to the barracks, walking through the darkness as steadily as any horse in the Roman army, I knew that my master was right.

8

THE DAWN CHORUS

It was very dark in the garden, which was not surprising, for it was still an hour before dawn. From deep inside the trees, I could hear rustles and twitterings. I came out of my nest and stood at the end of a branch.

'What about a rousing chorus to welcome the day?' I said.

There was no answer.

'Come on now, I know you're all awake.'

The rustlings stopped.

'What's the point of welcoming the day?' came a voice from one of the trees.

I sighed. 'Look, I know it was very sad when they killed Jesus. We were right not to sing yesterday as a mark of respect, especially as his body's in the tomb in our garden. But life must go on, mustn't it? Birds have always sung at dawn, so surely we should sing?'

But no one had any heart for singing. I didn't really feel like it myself, although, as song thrush and leader of the dawn chorus in the garden, I was, I suppose, in charge.

I tried once more. 'Jesus would have wanted us to sing. If he *was* the Son of God, as people are saying, he wouldn't have wanted us to sit on our nests and mope. Didn't God create us to give pleasure with our singing?'

'*You* might be able to sing with a broken heart,' said the sparrow. '*I* can't.'

I couldn't answer that.

'*Why* did they kill him?' asked the chaffinch.

'Because he was good,' said the owl, who was flying restlessly from tree to tree. 'He was so good, he showed them up. Especially the priests.'

'Why?'

'They were meant to be good but often weren't.'

'And they were jealous of him,' said the sparrow. 'Because people loved him.'

'They'd travel for miles to see him,' said the lark. 'I used to watch them. Then they'd wait for hours just to catch sight of him.'

'I was there when he fed thousands of people with just five small loaves and two fish,' said the sparrow.

'Why did he do that?' asked the chaffinch.

'Because they were hungry and there weren't any markets nearby.'

'There was even food left over for us,' said another sparrow. 'For we were hungry too.'

'Never mind *why* he did it,' I said impatiently. 'What I want to know is *how* did he do it? I mean, five loaves and two fish would scarcely feed a family of birds, let alone all those people. It's just not possible.'

'It was a miracle,' said the first sparrow.

I didn't believe in miracles. I was a solid, down-to-earth bird who led the dawn chorus and didn't believe in anything I couldn't see with my own two eyes or peck with my beak.

'Once I saw Jesus heal a man who couldn't speak,' said the wren. 'He just laid his hands on him and the man began to talk.'

'And I saw him give a blind man his sight,' said the lark.

'A poor woman touched the hem of his robe and was made well,' a blue tit added.

'He loved poor people,' said the lark.

'He loved *all* people,' said the sparrow. 'He cared for them. Didn't he say that they were like sheep without a shepherd?'

'I can't think why he loved them,' I said. 'Look what they did to him.'

'Even if he'd known that they would turn on him

and kill him, he wouldn't have stopped loving,' said the sparrow thoughtfully. 'That was just the way he was.'

I lifted my head and sniffed the air. The wind was changing. It would soon be day.

'Aren't any of you going to sing?' I asked. They all ignored me.

'What I remember best are the things Jesus said,' reflected the owl. 'He was very wise but he put things so simply, everyone could understand.'

'Like the time he said that not one sparrow is forgotten by God,' said the sparrow.

'And when he said that the most important thing in the world was for people to love God and love each other,' said the owl.

'If only they'd done that, they wouldn't have killed him,' said the wren sadly.

'Or treated him so badly,' added the lark. 'What was it he said? "Foxes have holes and birds have their nests, but I have nowhere to lie down and rest." '

Everyone fell silent. I looked towards the east and could see the first glimmer of dawn.

'It'll be light soon,' I said.

'It'll never be light,' said the sparrow sadly. 'Not now they've killed God's own Son.'

'Look, all this talk is all very well,' I said. 'But it's not going to bring Jesus back, is it? I mean he was a good man, a holy man, but it's over now and we have to get on with our lives. So how about a rousing chorus to start the day?'

There was silence.

'You don't believe he was God's Son, do you?' asked the lark.

'No,' I said. 'I suppose not.'

'But what about all the things he did? The miracles he performed.'

'*I* didn't see any of them,' I said stubbornly. 'If I'd seen a miracle I might feel the same as you. As it is,

I just don't see the point of it. Why would God send his Son to earth in the first place?'

'Because he wanted to show people that he was close to them,' said the sparrow. 'That he understood them.'

'And that he loved them,' added the owl.

'So why did God let him die then?' I persisted.

No one could answer that.

'Perhaps,' the sparrow said at last, 'perhaps he died so that people would be forgiven for the bad things they'd done.'

Everyone was quiet. I suddenly felt very tired, for I hadn't been able to sleep for two days, not since they had brought Jesus' body to the garden, laid it in the tomb and rolled a great stone across the entrance to seal it. Two Roman soldiers had been left on guard and the noise of their feet stamping up and down all night would have kept any self-respecting bird awake.

Perhaps, I thought, the soldiers would go away once daylight came. Perhaps, after a meal of worms, life would go on as it had before. Perhaps, with the coming of a new day, this dreadful heaviness we all felt would lift, and we would be able to welcome the dawn with song.

Or perhaps we would never be able to sing again.

But that wouldn't do. I didn't believe in moping.

Do something positive if you're sad, like clean out your nest, or stretch your wings—that's what my mother taught me when I was still a fledgling.

'It's getting lighter,' I said, in an encouraging voice.

No one spoke. Suddenly it was silent in the garden. There was no sound of the soldiers. Perhaps they've gone, I thought hopefully. I listened. Then I heard footsteps, light and hesitating. They were coming towards us. I peered over the top of my nest. It was a woman. I could just make out her dark shape passing under the trees.

She reached the tomb and stopped. I heard her draw in her breath. For a moment she stayed absolutely still, then she turned and ran away.

I flew down to the tomb.

The great stone had been rolled to one side and the entrance was open!

I flew inside.

And flew straight out again, shaking with fright, for there, in the tomb, were two strange figures. They looked like people but had wings, great white wings! They shone with radiant light and in that light I could see a heap of linen cloths. They were the cloths in which Jesus' body had been wrapped. There was no sign of Jesus.

'What's happened?' asked the sparrow as I returned

to my tree, but I was so shaken I couldn't speak.

'He's not there,' I said at last.

'What you mean, "He's not there"? He *must* be there. What's happened to the soldiers?'

'They've gone.'

'So no one's there at all?'

'Yes,' I said. 'There are two… there are two…'

'Two what?'

'People, but with wings like birds,' I said. 'They were shining…'

'They sound like angels,' said the sparrow.

'But they can't be. I don't believe in angels.'

I flew back to the tomb.

The woman had returned. She was just inside the entrance, tears pouring down her face.

'They have taken my Lord away, and I don't know where they have put him!'

'Why are you looking in a tomb for someone who is alive?' asked one of the angels.

The other stood up. 'Jesus is not here. He has risen from the dead, just as he promised he would.'

The woman stared at them. She was so upset I don't think she took in what they were saying.

There was a noise from the far end of the garden. A man was approaching. It was still too dark to see his face, but I thought he must be the gardener.

'Why are you crying?' the man asked her gently.

'Who are you looking for?'

She turned and ran towards him. 'If you have taken him, sir, tell me where he is.'

The man came closer.

'Mary,' he said.

And at that moment a ray of sunshine fell across the man's face and I saw him clearly for the first time.

'It's Jesus!' called the sparrow.

'Master!' Mary cried.

And as daylight flooded the garden, I bowed my

head, for at last, I too, believed that Jesus was God's Son. That he was special. That he had risen from his grave and was alive again! That he was the Lord of everything!

I flapped my wings and soared high into the air.

'Come on now, birds,' I called. 'Let's give a rousing chorus, for there never was a better dawn! Let's welcome the new day and the risen Lord!'

We raised our voices and, although I say so myself, it was the best dawn chorus there has *ever* been.

THE END, AND THE BEGINNING...

With the coming of day, the birds in the garden rose up and, still singing, they flew out over the land.

In the stable in the army barracks just outside Jerusalem, the Roman horse heard the message of hope from the lark as he was being saddled up for another day's work. He threw up his head and neighed to his companion, and soon all the horses in the stables were neighing and whinnying so loudly that their masters came running to see what all the fuss was about.

The song thrush flew over the chief priest's house and sang the good news to the cockerel, who stood on the courtyard wall and crowed even louder than before, to the delight of his admiring hens. Perhaps, thought the cockerel, Peter would soon hear the news and be comforted.

The mouse in the garden of Gethsemane ran for

cover when he saw the owl swooping overhead. But the owl, who should have been asleep long since, was not tired, neither was he hunting for food as he told of the miracle that had occurred. And the mouse was so happy that he ran round the garden telling the news to all his new friends.

The cat was feeding her kittens when the little wren perched on the tree outside her hiding-place in Jerusalem and burst into song. She hurried to tell her friend who lived down the road. For once, *she* would be first with the news.

And as the sun climbed higher in the sky, the message was passed from bird to bird and animal to animal.

The pigeon, who had been freed by Jesus, heard the news as he flew high over the Temple walls. He was so amazed he almost swallowed the juicy worm he was carefully carrying in his beak. He quickly flew to his new nest on the outskirts of the city to give his wife the news, but was soon off again—for she was busy keeping two fine eggs safe and warm and he had to provide her with food.

And so the news travelled further and further, beyond the city of Jerusalem to the surrounding villages and farms. And the little donkey, deep in conversation with his friend the camel about what a *real* king was like, heard the good news on his farm at

Bethphage near the Mount of Olives. So did his mother, toiling in the fields, who spared a thought for Jesus' own mother, who she had carried on her back so many years earlier.

Still further the news travelled, to villages, towns and cities throughout Judaea. And in Jericho the old dog, running beside his master, heard it and barked loudly, wagging his tail.

And the birds took the news to the fish of the ocean and it was carried over the seas to other lands until everyone had heard about Jesus:

—the healer,

—the king,

—the saviour,

—the servant,

—the man,

—the prophet,

—the Son of God,

—who rose from the dead,

—the friend of every living creature in the world.